STEP INTO READING

reading

Barbie™

Little Lost Dolphin

THIS BOOK BELONGS TO

your name here!

3 of my *favorite* books

① ....

② ....

③ ....

Here is a picture of **me** after I finish a **great** book!

Dear Parent:

Congratulations! Your child is taking the first steps on an exciting journey. The destination? Independent reading!

STEP INTO READING® will help your child get there. The program offers five steps to reading success. Each step includes fun stories and colorful art. There are also Step into Reading Sticker Books, Step into Reading Math Readers, Step into Reading Phonics Readers, Step into Reading Write-In Readers, and Step into Reading Phonics Boxed Sets—a complete literacy program with something for every child.

Learning to Read, Step by Step!

Ready to Read   Preschool–Kindergarten
• big type and easy words • rhyme and rhythm • picture clues
For children who know the alphabet and are eager to begin reading.

Reading with Help   Preschool–Grade 1
• basic vocabulary • short sentences • simple stories
For children who recognize familiar words and sound out new words with help.

Reading on Your Own   Grades 1–3
• engaging characters • easy-to-follow plots • popular topics
For children who are ready to read on their own.

Reading Paragraphs   Grades 2–3
• challenging vocabulary • short paragraphs • exciting stories
For newly independent readers who read simple sentences with confidence.

Ready for Chapters   Grades 2–4
• chapters • longer paragraphs • full-color art
For children who want to take the plunge into chapter books but still like colorful pictures.

STEP INTO READING® is designed to give every child a successful reading experience. The grade levels are only guides. Children can progress through the steps at their own speed, developing confidence in their reading, no matter what their grade.

Remember, a lifetime love of reading starts with a single step!

For Ella and Ava—K.L.D.
For SJ Kwon—J.A.

STEP INTO READING®

STEP 2

Barbie™

Little Lost Dolphin

By Kristen L. Depken

Illustrated by Jiyoung An

Random House 🏠 New York

Barbie lives
by the ocean.

She loves
to swim!

Barbie also loves
to ride her Jet Ski.
She likes to go fast!

She rides
to a lagoon.
She hears a noise.
Squeak! Squeak!

It is a baby dolphin!
He is swimming
in the lagoon, too.

Barbie waves hello.

The dolphin is lost.

He cannot find
his family.

Barbie comforts
the baby dolphin.
She will help him
find his family!

Barbie gets
on her Jet Ski.

Barbie and the dolphin
search all around
the lagoon.

They see fish
and birds
and seaweed.
But they do not see
the dolphin's family.

It is getting dark.
The dolphin is sad.
Barbie has
to go home.

The dolphin does not
want her to go.

The baby dolphin
follows Barbie home!

Barbie calls
a dolphin expert.
She tells Barbie how
to care for the dolphin.

Barbie feeds
the dolphin
from a bottle.

Barbie sets up a tent.
She will watch
the dolphin.

Barbie pats him
on the head.
She says good night.

The baby dolphin

gets a good

night's sleep!

The next day,
Barbie's friends
come over.
The dolphin jumps!

He plays with them
and has fun!
But he misses
his family.

Barbie and her friends
will look for
the dolphin's family.
They ride Jet Skis.

The dolphin swims
next to them.
They look
near the lagoon.

They look

near a cove.

They cannot find
the dolphin's family!
They hear a noise.
<u>Squeak! Squeak!</u>

It is the baby
dolphin's family!
He could not find them.
But <u>they</u> found <u>him</u>!

The dolphins jump
and splash
and play.

Barbie and her friends
watch the dolphin family
play together.

Soon it is time
to go home.
The dolphins thank
Barbie for her help.

Barbie waves goodbye
to the baby dolphin.
She is so happy
to have a new friend!